IVOR the engine
Ivor's Birthday

Story by OLIVER POSTGATE
Pictures by PETER FIRMIN

It was Ivor's birthday.

Well, it may have been. Nobody knows when Ivor's birthday is, so Mr Dinwiddy chooses the first really fine day in Spring and makes Ivor a birthday cake.

Well, you might call it a cake, but it looked very nasty. The only way you could tell it was a birthday cake was by reading the green words, HAPPY BIRTHDAY IVOR, which Mr Dinwiddy had written on its grey and purple top. It certainly did not look good to eat but you couldn't have eaten it if you had tried, because it was hard as stone, being made of coal dust mixed with cement and gunpowder and chopped roman candles.

Ivor hooted with joy when he saw it. He loved his birthday cake.

Ivor didn't exactly *eat* his birthday cake. Mr Dinwiddy just popped it into his fire on top of the coal. Nothing happened for a moment and then, with a roar and a crackle, clouds of bright green smoke full of purple, pink and pale blue flashes billowed up from his funnel. Everybody cheered and Eli Bevan

the baker brought up his present for Ivor.

Eli's present was the same every year, a batch of freshly baked rolls shaped like little railway engines. Ivor hooted when he saw them and everybody in Llaniog knew it was time to run to the station to share Ivor's birthday breakfast.

Ivor loved his birthday but his was
different from yours or mine. Being a
railway engine, he did not really want to be
given presents. What he liked best of all was
giving presents to other people. Jones and
Eli were busy buttering and handing out the
hot rolls and everybody was very happy.

Well, nearly everybody. Dai Station the station-master was looking glum, as usual.

"I don't think much of birthdays," he said, "people giving each other presents and that. I think it's a bit silly. And as for railway engines having birthdays ... that's just ridiculous! I shall be glad when it is over!"

Dai stumped away to count up the used
tickets just as another lot of Ivor's friends
turned up on their bicycles. This was the
Grumbly and District Choral Society who
had come to help Ivor with his day's work.

They hooked on the trucks, loaded them
with goods and sat on top.

POOP POOP ... went Ivor's whistle.

CHUFF...CHUFF...CHUFF, CHUFF, CHUFF, away they went, and as they went they sang and waved and laughed together as the green smoke blew all around and away up into the sky.

The sun shone happily on them as they puffed along the line, over the hill, past the coal mine and up to the posh house where

Mrs Porty lives.

Mrs Porty was waiting for them. She had a present for Ivor, a huge present, all done up with coloured paper and ribbons.

The choral society jumped down and very carefully ... so as not to tear the paper or spoil the ribbon ... they opened the parcel. In the parcel was the biggest, woolliest pullover in the whole world. It must have

been knitted from woollen rope on needles
the size of broom-handles!

It fitted Ivor perfectly. It might have been
made for him. Well, of course, it *was* made
for him, wasn't it! Nobody else in the world is
quite that shape.

"There!" said Mrs Porty. "That will keep
you warm and cosy, Ivor!"

POOP-POOP...went Ivor's whistle.

That evening, after all the laughing and
singing and dancing was over, Ivor stood at
Llaniog Station wearing his new pullover.
Jones and Dai were sitting on his step, with
Nell, Mr Pugh's sheepdog.

"Do you think Ivor's birthday is over
now?" asked Dai.

"I don't know!" laughed Jones. "When do

birthdays end?"

"Well, I think birthdays for railway engines is silly!" said Dai. "We'll be having birthdays for sheep next!"

"Why not?" asked Jones.

"Because ... because ..." Dai couldn't think of a reason ... "because sheep are all the same."

"That one isn't," said Jones pointing to one
lamb which was standing by itself. "I have
been watching that one and it has no mother.
Isn't that right, Nell?"

Nell is a very clever sheepdog. She knew
what to do. She rounded up the lonely lamb,
drove it down to Ivor, gently lifted it in her
mouth and placed it on Ivor's step.

Jones laughed. "No! That is a birthday present which Ivor will not accept! He is wearing a woolly pullover, but that doesn't mean he is a mother sheep!"

Nell whimpered and looked at Dai.

"Somebody will have to look after it," said Dai. "Lambs need warm milk."

"That's right," said Jones, looking at Dai.

Jones and Nell went on looking at Dai until he spoke. "All right," he said. "I'll look after it."

Nell wagged her tail and licked the tip of Dai's nose.

The next morning Jones the Steam came to work as usual. Well, not quite as usual. Ivor was wearing his huge woolly pullover and in the booking office Dai was trying to feed a bottle of warm milk to the lamb.

"Oh Dai, you're a funny-looking mother sheep!" laughed Jones.

Dai did not laugh. "Not half as funny as Ivor looks, wearing that silly pullover," he

said crossly.

"Hush, Dai," whispered Jones, "Ivor is very sensitive about how he looks."

"Never mind about that," grunted Dai. "You and Ivor are here to work. You might as well get on with it. Ivor's birthday is over now."

"I wonder if it is..." thought Jones. Jones loaded up the goods and he and Ivor

set off on their day's work. Jones could feel that Ivor was worried about something but he didn't find out what it was until they had delivered Mr Hannibal his ploughshare and Mr Davies his tomatoes.

They rolled down the hill past the schoolhouse at playtime. As usual the children ran to the fence to shout and wave to Ivor. But this time, when they saw him in

his woolly pullover they laughed. Oh how
they laughed … "Bah bah! Who's a silly
sheep then? … Baaah Baah."

They laughed and bleated but Ivor took no
notice. He steamed past, trying to look as
dignified as possible, which is not easy when
you are dressed up as a sheep, but the
moment he was round the corner and out of
sight …

PSSSST...BONK PSSST, BONK-BONK...he slammed on all his brakes.

Jones the Steam climbed down.

"Perhaps that pullover is a bit too warm for you, Ivor," he suggested. "After all, you don't feel the cold because you have a big fire in your middle, so maybe I could take it off. How about that?"

POOP POOP POOPETY POOP POOP... Ivor
thought that was a good idea.

Jones rolled up the pullover and put a rope
around it.

"The trouble with presents is that you
can't just give them back," he said. "Mrs
Porty went to a lot of trouble knitting this.
She made it to keep you warm, but as you
don't need to be kept warm I suppose it
would be all right for us to give it to
somebody who does ... but who on earth
would it fit? I don't know!"

POOP POOP POOPETY POOP POOOP POOP. Ivor
knew!

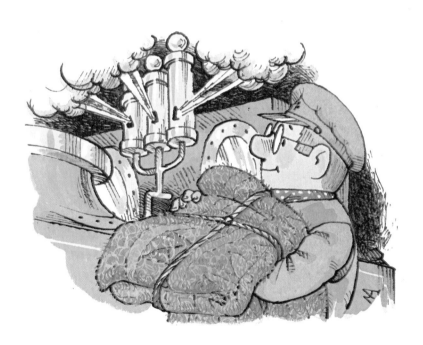

"Come on then, show me!" shouted Jones.
He jumped into the cab and off they went.
Ivor took him to Llanmad where Charlie
Banger's Circus stays in winter.

"It's for Alice!" shouted Jones. "Of course!
She feels the cold terribly!"

Alice, as you know, or have guessed, was
an elephant. She was a very old friend. So
was Bani, the elephant-keeper.

With a bit of adjustment the pullover fitted
Alice perfectly.

"Oh you are a beautiful English elephant!"
cried Bani. "What shall we give to Ivor in
return?"

Bani and Alice gave Ivor a huge glittering
elephant's necklace. It looked very good on
Ivor's tank.

POOP POOPETY POOOP...Ivor was pleased.

When Mrs Porty saw Ivor's necklace she
clapped her hands. "That is beautiful!" she
cried. "May I try it on?"

The necklace was so big she had to fold it
twice. It hung on her like a giant mayor's
chain and it looked magnificent.

"It is too good for Ivor to wear all the
time," said Jones. "The rain would spoil it. I

am sure Ivor would like you to keep it for
him. I think Alice would too."

"Alice? Who is Alice?" asked Mrs Porty.

So Jones told Mrs Porty about the pullover
and how Alice feels the cold. Mrs Porty did
not mind at all. She seemed pleased.

"I shall look after the necklace for you,"
she announced.

On the way home Jones wondered
whether Ivor's birthday was really over now
but when they reached Llaniog, Dai was
nowhere to be seen.

In the end Jones found him in the field,
trying to show the lamb how to eat grass.

"Oh what hard work it is, being a mother!"
laughed Jones.

Dai did not laugh. "Some of us take our
responsibilities seriously," he said proudly.

In fact Dai's responsibilities grew more
and more serious as the weeks went by. The
lamb was very playful. It also grew up into a
young ram who enjoyed butting into things.
Nell the sheepdog came by now and then to
make sure it was all right. It was all right,
but nothing else was. It pushed over the
boxes, ate the tickets, spilt the teapot, broke
pieces off the doors and bent the pipes.

Dai loved it so much that he didn't seem to notice but Mrs Porty, who really owns the whole railway, came along to find out what was happening.

Dai Station was there and he was pleased to see her. The ram was there too, but he was not pleased to see her. In fact he decided that

she was about to leave. He decided to help
her on her way. He lowered his head and
charged. Mrs Porty did not wait. She
scuttled back to her donkey-cart and was
helped into it by the ram.

"Get rid of it!" she shouted. "Send it back
to where it came from!"

Dai stood there quite amazed. I don't think
he quite knew what had happened, but Nell
the sheepdog knew. She knew it was time to
round up the ram and put him back with the
other sheep. So that is what she did.

That evening, Jones and Dai sat on Ivor's